meera

DEB

Copyright © 2024 by Deb

All rights reserved.

This book or any portion thereof may not be reproduced or used in any manner whatsoever without the express written permission of the respective writer of the respective content except for the use of brief quotations in a book review.

The writer of the respective work holds sole responsibility for the originality of the content and The Write Order is not responsible in any way whatsoever.

Printed in India

ISBN: 978-93-95563-65-9

First Printing, 2024

The Write Order
A division of Nasadiya Technologies Private Ltd.
Koramangala, Bengaluru
Karnataka-560029

THE WRITE ORDER PUBLICATIONS.

www.thewriteorder.com

Typeset by MAP Systems, Bengaluru

Book Cover designed by Vani Chandra

Publishing Consultant - Nandini

Acknowledgments

Wow, this is surreal!

I mean, who would have ever imagined that the boy who once aspired to be a scientist but was haunted by nightmares from Physics and faced failure in his 11th-standard exams would eventually transform into a published author? Well, truth be told, a few individuals did anticipate it, and while they recognize themselves, it's fair to express my gratitude.

Arpita, you have been an unwavering pillar of support from way back, guiding me through challenging times and ultimately helping me bring this achievement to fruition. There's truly nothing more remarkable than having someone steadfastly by your side.

Niket, my publisher, you've turned my dream into reality. The notion of someone approaching me to publish my writing seemed like a distant thought (alright, perhaps I entertained it once or twice!), but you've made it a concrete accomplishment.

Chitralekha, ma'am, you were the first to discern that the young lad scribbling in his diary held potential, and your initial constructive feedback played an integral role. Without you, I might not have embarked on this writing journey.

Maa, your support means the world. Not just confined to this book, but your consistent encouragement to follow my heart has been a driving force.

To my friends Amrit, Ahnnik, Mayank, and Rishi, you were among the first to back me vocally. And though my dearest friend Sudatta rarely delves into my writing, his place in my heart remains irreplaceable.

A special note of gratitude to my buddy bro Moi for, well, you know what.

Last but certainly not least, my Instagram followers – it's your immense love and patience that made all of this possible. Each one of you who tirelessly read, liked, shared my stories, and brought Meera to life, I owe you a debt of gratitude.

This privilege is bestowed upon only a select few, and it's all due to the kindness and generosity you've showered upon me.

For Baba.

Contents

Acknowledgments vii

leaning in 1
closer 21
more 35
breathless 49
catching 59
falling 69
moans 81
louder 93
stop 103
again 113
silence 125
goosebumps 137
cuddles 145

leaning in

[1]

meera and i have been seeing each other for a while now. seeing each other in terrible sexts, and on nights so lonely that we cling to each other like star-crossed lovers when love is often the last thing on our minds. i wake up before she does and leave before she can stop me. she knows i am afraid of attachments, and sometimes i sense something similar inside her.

i have become so familiar with meera in bed that i often forget to switch the lights off, even on nights when she is traveling in a far-off land, probably sleeping her way out of love like me. she likes to keep the lights on.

falling short of words during conversations is something we both have in common, so we browse the internet in search of everything they call intellectual.

starry night by van gogh is strangely still the only thing we collectively like to look at when looking for things to talk about; strange because when we are tearing each other apart, there is so much we say to each other in between the silences and the sighs. amidst the moans and the melancholy, she kisses me a little longer to tell me how much she misses her man.

yesterday, she drunk-texted me saying that she wanted me to pick her up from a place in paris, but before i could answer, i got another text, possibly from a friend, that said that she was fine. i do not know if i really needed to know. i will tell her the next time we meet.

"it's over before it started." she would say.

"isn't that how love should be?"

***

[2]

i never thought i would fall in love again, i say. meera doesn't say anything, but there is something about the way she smiles every time i say it. she doesn't feel the same, she says, and we go about doing what we always do. it's just so easy doing things with her; long drives down that supposedly haunted street, scaring couples making out with noises that probably scare the ghosts too, if any, before getting home with a couple of kulfis and having sex.

weekends like these are something i have almost gotten used to, and now that i see her working late on weekdays, not remembering to check if i was fine, i remember one of our first conversations. we had met at a friend's place – a friend we both secretly hated – and she was just trying to get over this guy she had left her house for. "i don't want another relationship," i remember saying and getting only that smile in return. we went home that night and started what i had thought would be 'just another fling'.

some nights i wish that were true, but sometimes, when i see the neon lights from the streets; when i see them fall upon her face, and her eyes just staring at the endlessness of all that exists, without any expression, i know.

"meera?" i say.

"…"

"do you…?"

"remember what you said the first time we hooked up?"

during such conversations, meera tells me about this one man she loved. she tells me about how he broke into her defenses, made her tattoo his name on her heart, and left. "you know, people don't want to love," she says, her eyes moist with a memory she thought she had buried, "they want to have people love them."

last night, when we were watching lost in translation, meera asked me the same thing charlotte asks bob: "does it get easier?" she knew the answer. "no," she said before asking me to kiss her again.

"maybe you did," meera says, "maybe you did think about falling for me, but never did."

"how…can you say that?"

"you are still here."

✳✳✳

[3]

"when is it that you realize there's no end to this loneliness?"

from across the table in a café we happened to chance across, she asks me a question i have no clue about. meera talks to me about things that make her sad, and i stare at her wondering if i am one of them. it's been a little while since we made eye contact.

i don't think i would ever understand meera. no, don't get me wrong. i would always be strangely, madly in love with the idea of her inside my head; fidgeting with the half-empty cup in her lap and staring at me with something that closely resembles longing. it didn't take much for me to realize that it wasn't quite my fault.

all the sad things that had happened to her before me, i could do little to change that.

and it wasn't like she was not good with people. she was just…not comfortable enough to share a part of her with them.

but she would often call me up during nights, from the other side of the bed, asking me how i was and if i loved her yet. she never waited for an answer. she would disconnect and make quiet love to me, probably almost making sure that i didn't find her crazy.

"deb?" meera jumps me out of the reverie. "i think you are getting a call."

on the phone display: 'meera calling.'

✱✱✱

[4]

"won't you rather wait for the right one instead of giving up on love?"

we have been sitting here for a while now, looking at the chaos from afar, as the silence grows louder than the noise and emptiness takes the wheel. "you love talking about love, don't you?" meera asks, almost at the risk of sounding like an insult, and adds, "but you do write well."

our discussion on everything ends with me agreeing to the fact that she understands life more, and somehow, today, it feels like she has given up. her fingers caress the inside of my palms, as we look in different directions and think about vaguely different things.

"would you ever write about me?" she sounds hopeful for a moment before i shake my head. the moonlight is merely not enough to make us see each other, but i can feel the growing sense of sadness between us.

she answers, "you know, deb, many people spend their entire lives in search of love, people like you write about; i don't think everyone gets that."

"it's almost as if, you don't want to see all the love you get from the few people you let in, you have the tendency to ignore everything they feel about you. you grieve about loneliness when there are people who care."

she looks at me for a moment, gets up, and leaves.

***

[5]

"you know there are days when you don't have things to say to people?"

"like when you wanna cuddle and watch old mushy movies? when you just forget everything and believe in love?"

"sex would be good too."

"and pizza!"

"and ice cream."

"deb?"

"yeah?"

"why do you believe in love?"

meera has this strange habit of asking me questions that we often argue over and over again. sometimes, it makes me believe that she just likes to counter everything i say and that she actually is someone who secretly wants us to have a crazy love story.

i think one of these days, when she is done arguing about how love is a myth, she is going to tell me about everything she has ever kept from me, including how she stays awake every night just to watch me sleep. she does these little things sometimes that keeps me hoping that maybe someday, just someday, meera and i are going to be together.

"aren't we together already?" she asks, probably sensing the reason for my silence.

"are we?"

she punches me in the arm and tells me that i think too much about inconsequential things. laughingly, i ask her if she would like me ever to go around falling in love with somebody else. "as long as you aren't doing it to forget me."

"maybe i should."

"i don't think you can."

"of course, i can, meera. i am not spending my life thinking about somebody who doesn't…"

"you believe in that shit, deb. you believe in love."

✳✳✳

[6]

i met this girl at anand's party last night. the first time i saw her was when she was in the middle of a discussion that was seemingly boring her to death. she was wearing a cami dress, burgundy in color.

we saw each other from a distance and smiled at the absurdness of being among people who we had no business around. a few minutes later, she came up to me.

"meera," she said and put out a hand.

i realized i had been staring at her for too long.

"d-deb."

in the next couple of hours, we talked about everything ranging from stephen king to the futility of human life. but for the most part, we had been quiet. with a glass each in our hands, we stood at the balcony and let the moments pass by, not wanting to rush through, like almost whispering but to time itself that we had it in plenty.

"for a writer, you are awfully short of words," she had said in between, laughing.

"and for someone who said she loves the silences, you are strangely impatient."

"would you like to come home?"

not much was said until after we were done doing the deed at her place. but long after it was over, she continued to hold me tight, almost telling me in her own lack of words that she needed me to hold her back.

"why do people leave? why is it never enough?"

"u-uh, i think i should go, meera."

chuckling, she let go of me. "scared, are you? don't be. love is the last thing on my mind."

yet, it was hard not to notice her eyes in the dark.

"i don't think they do," i remember saying while getting off the bed.

"what do you mean?"

"i don't think people leave, meera. maybe they just.. stop loving us the way they used to."

***

[7]

"people talk about the right ones so much and yet end up with the wrong ones all their life."
"aren't you being too harsh on people, meera?"
"..."
"i mean, it's all about asking for love," she lowers herself to sleep on my lap.
"but what if there wasn't a right one - for you, for me, for any of us?"
"you don't think there is a right one somewhere for you?"
"i don't."
"i think you do," i say, caressing the strands of hair falling over her face.
"maybe, when i was younger."
"..."
"failed relationships, some personal and some not; they make you stop believing."
"if you did, you know...find the right one, would you stay?"
"i guess, i will."
"why?"
"doesn't hurt to love, be loved, and not fail at it for once."

***

[8]

"it is a great privilege to love someone and have them love you back," she says.
"stop copying dear old augustus, would you?"
she laughs and goes on to tell me about her first day at work. meera and i talk almost every day now. i don't quite know if she feels the same way that i do. it scares me a little.
from a hundred time zones away, she tells me about things so mundane that you'd wonder why she is stretching this second into a few thousand more, keeping me on the other end of what is only a beating heart.
"i'm scared too," she says, somehow reading my thoughts, and goes quiet after.
the silence here is not quite comforting. she knows it too and is now fiddling with the little bracelet her mother had left behind.
in the little time that we have known each other, meera and i share this incredible something that each of us knows about but neither wants to say. perhaps not just to the other person, but even to our own selves.
for all our talk about love and longing, it is only just empty palms that we have left each other with when it was time.

"did you fall asleep?"

she has not. but i do not know how else to stop this. this longing that only expands with every song we share.

"almost," she whispers.

"what about the love that doesn't come back, the kind that only departs, and never lands?"

she stays quiet for some time, and answers, "you let it go."

***

[9]

"it gets difficult," says meera.

if we ever get to a point where we are together, i hope to tell her that i don't like how ambiguous she is sometimes. but right now, the last ferry of the evening is what we are waiting for. she is busy with her new lens, taking pictures of a monument that sees thousands of people like us every day. nomads, wandering across this city lost in a civilization balancing itself between what it wants and what it must become.

"every day, i have this feeling that something is being taken away from me, and it's almost like i am letting it."

"why is that a bad thing?"

the ferry is here, and meera helps me get on. i have a mild, completely unfounded fear of falling off boats. there are several others, even first-timers overawed by the sheer feeling of being on one. "i think we stress too much on the idea of first times," she says, responding to my obvious but cheesy remark on how this is also our first time together here.

i shake my head, smiling, and stare at her clicking pictures of what is now a tinge of orange over a blanket of black clouds. suddenly, she points the camera at me and clicks what i believe must be another terrible version of me.

she comes closer, keeps it aside, and rests her head on my shoulders.

"you know, i never thought we'd be here, talking as we are, making plans to meet again."

"and why do you need to plan everything, deb?"

maybe it is that unfounded fear of drowning. we both stare at each other, unsure of where this could go; two people close together, and yet, with an underlying sense of invisible distance. does she also feel the same way when i talk about our differences? she says she hasn't thought about it yet.

the dusk is about to retract itself. the night is not so far. she has a smile on her face when we exit the ferry. she asks, "if, you know, you could choose between us never meeting and meeting a person you matched a hundred per cent with, what would you do?"

"i'd think my cheesiness is brushing off on you."

***

closer

[1]

"i saw my mother die," meera says, "and i felt no remorse."

after downing a few pegs, she opens up about things keeping her awake on winter mornings and she has had more than a few tonight.

"you know, they l-lie. they lie when they talk about loss."

"..."

"why the fuck are you so quiet?"

i smile and lie back on the bed, waiting for her ramble to go on.

"they talk about how it hits you so hard and you are forced to cry your heart out. i call bullshit. i didn't cry when my mom decided to die."

"not everyone experiences pain the same way you do, meera."

"why can't they? why can't they feel the same way?"

"this is not about them, is it?"

somehow, even before asking the question, i had a feeling that it will touch a nerve.

"i want him to suffer, alright? would that suffice?"

meera was still getting over her past. it was something that she had made clear well before we started dating. i could sometimes understand exactly how meera was feeling.

sometimes, i could not. it had taken me a while, but i had come to realize that she wasn't intending to let go.

"i love you," she says, with a near sense of regret and remorse.

"it's okay…you don't have to."

"why do you keep up with all this – why?"

smiling, i shake my head. i didn't know. "do you need a hug?" i ask, watching her tremble.

"fuck off, alright? just…fuck off."

and just like that, meera begins to cry.

***

[2]

i am dying. meera doesn't know.
over a cup of tea and a glass of mojito, i plan to tell her about the growing tumour in my lungs.
"so," she begins, "tell me?"
i am still pondering over it. would it be right to tell her that i only have a few more months to wait? would she be willing to lie about this love knowing that this person, who can not see a future with her, be gone soon?
"you look beautiful," i say, smiling, trying hard not to cry.
"tell me something i don't know."
we laugh aloud, almost forgetting for a moment that there are strangers sitting.
"is this about making you wait?"
meera keeps going back to it, unlike me, who, until i found out about the time i had left, had given up on an answer. i didn't need one. it was enough to know that there was something between us that was still breathing. i didn't need to know whether she would stay forever. nobody does.
"are you hiding something?"
i shake my head.
it's been long since meera said that she loved me. she says she doesn't want to.

but sometimes, when she makes these invisible patterns on my palm, looking out the window, i can sense the calm that shrouds us for a little while. and on her lips, an unsung melody plays itself, waiting perhaps, for the storm to pass.

"meera?"

"deb?"

"remember what margo said about paper towns and paper people?"

"that it's always uglier up close?"

"i think this love i have for you is paper too."

"..."

"but this paper love – i wanna hold it close. and for now, just for tonight, i want it to hold me back."

"just for tonight?"

"just for tonight."

***

[*3*]

it has been six months since they found a tumour in my lungs. meera is away on one of her trips.

"don't die without me," she had said, half-joking before she left. i hope i don't.

to get away from death, or maybe life, i decided to visit this hill station where everyone seems to know each other. there is only so much to do, so i make small talk with people who seem disinterested every time i tell them that i don't want to buy anything.

the only friend i had here was the owner of a large piece of land, now used to bury the dead. "call me stan," the old man had said during our first meet. stan and i had become friends because we were both what you can call a strange kind of lonely. he would have people coming in every day to meet him, pay their regards for helping them in some way, and go.

"the dead keeps me company," he would sometimes say, and then realize that it was probably too insensitive. "tell me about meera," he would ask, and every time i did, he would smile.

"why do you love meera?" he asked me once.

"never found a reason. never needed to."

"even i had a meera once."

he would go on to tell me about how it was on valentine's day that he had confessed, greeted by a smile and then tears. i looked at him, wondering if this was what would happen to meera when i was gone.

"what happened?"

"she was too precious to live," i thought i heard him say as he poured us tea.

"do you miss her, stan?"

"do you think meera would miss you?"

it was the wrong thing to ask. that night, when i was home, i got a call from him. i heard him cry, and before i could ask, he told me how he could never forget the way she looked at him the first time they made love, knowing all too well that it could be their last. it wasn't. she lived long enough to give him memories that lasted long.

a week later, stan died of a cardiac arrest.

a letter arrived the same day. it was from him, probably meant to reach me after he was dead.

there were photographs of him and her, with a note attached. it said: "leave something behind, deb. always leave something behind."

***

[4]

i miss him. i miss deb.

the doctor says he may have to stay at the hospital for a few months. it's hard to imagine seeing him die; see him slowly wither in front of my eyes. i know that might just be what happens but you know what they say about waiting for people, right? that they come back to you in some way if you love them hard enough?

i am counting on that.

he once told me that he loved sunflowers because everybody loved sunflowers. the little things that he does without telling anybody, and nobody really notices because he doesn't want them to, those are the things that make me want to question my decision-making ability.

deb has been in love with me for a long time. it's sad how some people never get the love they deserve because they end up loving the wrong person. but for all his selflessness, i am selfish. deep in my heart, i know well that this meera would never have another deb.

"why can't you, meera?" he had gently whispered this question to me one night.

i never had answers to his questions, only silence that he thought he could someday decipher.

maybe i was waiting for that one moment they keep telling us about when you know when you just know. i don't think you always need one.

when i think about him today, the only thing that i want is for him to live a little longer and i want to tell him that i was wrong; that i know. i want to tell him that i am going to stay and that he doesn't need to let go.

i wish to tell him that his meera is here.

***

[5]

"people are fools," she says, "they care too little for themselves."
"some people," i say, correcting her, with a careful emphasis on the first word.
"doesn't matter, does it?"
one of those days.
"deb?"
"meera?"
"would you forget me if i pack my bags and leave tonight?"
playing a john mayer song, i let the silence grow inside us.
she tells me she needs a cup of tea. i smile, and point to the right of her. it's already there.
one of these days, i am going to die. i know we all are, but you know how it is. i do not want to. a part of me wants to hold meera close for as long as i have left. a different, inhibited part wants me to let her go. i don't want her to hold on to me; hold on to my memories for too long.
sipping the overly sweetened tea, she hums a slow-moving tune, with a gentleness that i haven't noticed in meera before. her eyes are closed, and her breaths are heavy. a lump in her throat makes her stop.
she looks at me, not for too long, and says a few words that sound too close to something that she has always refrained from.

"meera?"

"deb?"

"people are fools," i say, "they care too little for themselves." smiling, she corrects me, "s-some people."

***

[6]

"we talk about everything, don't we?"

"if by that you are alluding to my sickness, meera, this conversation isn't going anywhere."

"why do we never talk about you - is there something that you don't like talking about?"

"let's just say my life wouldn't be one to read about if you ever picked up a random something at a bookstore."

in her silence, meera is probably thinking of what may be ailing her dying boyfriend. honestly, there isn't much to add to all that she already knows, except perhaps how i would hate to leave things behind when they finally seemed to have fallen into place.

"perhaps not, but your meera has always had a thing for things that seem out of place," she says and pulls a chair to come to hug me from behind.

"you smell nice."

"glad someone noticed," says meera, who has now rested a part of her face on my left shoulder.

even though there's so much unsaid in the things we say, our conversations always feel so complete. i sometimes wonder if that is a good thing. because given the lack of time, and this constant feeling of being a burden, i would rather let her know all that i have to.

"why have you been keeping up with this, meera?"

"keeping up with what?"

"this person who has been sick and a burden, knowing well that this investment is only going to yield negative returns?"

"is that what they taught you at business school?" her laughter makes me smile too.

"see there. that's what i keep up for. but then there's the good sex, terrible sense of humor, and a heart that beats for everybody but himself - the latter being quite literal at this point."

"so we are doing dead man jokes now, are we?"

"until the very end, my love."

"and then?"

"and then you write letters to me from beyond."

***

more

[1]

"i love you."

for the first time in a long time, meera tells me something that i have known since before she ever gave it a thought. one of those things she was careful enough to hide before the heart had had enough.

"why?"

i think the one thing people fear more than losing somebody they love is having to live with the regret of not being able to love enough when they had the chance. at some point, we have all been guilty of this; guilty of hiding what we felt for the fear of reciprocation and/or the lack of it.

meera looks at me from the other end of the room, sipping rosé, her face devoid of any expression.

i don't know how much more time it is going to take her to tell me all that she has to. "you already know everything you need to," she tells me when i ask, but sometimes, i wonder if we are running out of time.

a while later, meera, still holding that glass in her hand, comes closer and tells me that i need to believe her and before i can protest that i do, she holds my face and leans in.

"sloppy," she says after we are done. we both laugh and stare at each other at something that doesn't need to be talked about. something that we both know well enough for this love to lack words during nights that tread dangerously close to mornings.

handing me a leaf she picked from the street the first time we met, she says, "this is to your earlier question."

"..."

she then covers the palm holding the leaf with her own.

"why?"

***

[2]

"there are so many things in the world that wouldn't matter," says meera.

i am busy looking at the commotion on the street outside our house.

"did you hear what i said?"

"yes," i reply, absentminded.

there is silence from the other end and it takes me a while to realize that something is bothering her. i turn around to see meera sitting with her arms crossed and staring at the wall that has pictures of us. she does that when she has questions she is unwilling to ask.

"what is it this time?" i ask, moving to and beside her.

without saying anything, meera takes my hand in her own and holds it gently. she puts her head on my shoulder and asks me if i still loved her as much as i did before.

it's not a question she wants answered.

in a few seconds, when my palm begins to sweat, she lets it go.

smiling, "that's all it took for you to leave?" i ask.

she hits me on my arm and throws her arms up in the air.

"and about things not mattering, what do you mean?"

"this? us? love or whatever people call it? how is any of this going to matter?"

"doesn't mean we stop doing them."

"deb?"

"..."

"do you ever wonder how different things would be if we never met?"

there it was.

"then we would be with somebody else."

"you know, sometimes i would really prefer if you lied," she says and puts her arms around my shoulders.

for a few moments, she just holds me like that, quiet, unmoved.

"but then it wouldn't be us, would it?"

✳✳✳

[3]

people grieve in different ways. for my mother, it was spending hours near the idols she swore she could hear talking. for me, it's listening to nothing but my own silence for as long as it takes. but for meera, it was unlike anybody i had known.

"it's just death," she'd say.

it gave me a sense of security, knowing that she'd be just fine after i am gone. i didn't know how long i had left.

however, every time meera went to meet her father, she would return a different person. it almost felt like she brought back with her a part of him each time. her father, who had lost his wife years ago, not unlike so many of us, was still letting go. so, this time, i decided to accompany her.

"so you are…deb," he said and greeted me with a hug.

surrounding the dinner table that night was a strange sense of quiet. ever so often, the man would look up from his plate at me, then at his daughter, and smile.

perhaps, realizing that he was making me feel awkward, he said, "you know, deb, meera, and i have never been as close as i'd like. it's just so..wonderful to have you guys here tonight."

"whose fault is that, dad?" meera, who hadn't spoken a word since we arrived, said.

"it wasn't my fault that you decided to distance yourself from mum when she was alive. it wasn't mine when you decided to distance yourself from me after she died. it wasn't mine that i couldn't grieve when deb told me about..,"

there was little i could do at that moment. so, i left the two of them and waited outside while it rained. the crickets were quiet, the moon invisible. it was starting to get colder while i watched the drops come down upon the earth, changing the way it would smell. just like the people we love.

i found warmth on my shoulders. it was her father. "do you smoke?" he said, lighting a cigarette.

i shook my head and turned to leave when he called me back. "do you think it was my fault, deb?"

"it's really not my place to…"

"oftentimes, that's the only thing keeping us alive, you see."

"…"

"grief."

***

[4]

"why are humans so hard to understand?"
"not always."
"it's like, everyone wants a sky full of stars, everyone wants to see the bright night sky in all its glory, but nobody is willing to see them burn out and die, the stars."
meera and i were out on what she considers our first "official" date. we did not have a place in mind, and so, we decided to roam around the streets of this unknown city, hoping perhaps that our words would forever float around here somewhere, for us to come back to when we didn't have each other anymore.
"meera?"
she was walking right beside me, occasionally looking sideways, thinking about all the things she could ask me.
"do you want to kiss me?"
"h-here?"
laughing, she stopped. "you really don't know me, do you?"
for some reason, i wanted to tell her that it felt like i did. it felt like i had known her enough, enough to feel the way a heart feels when close to someone it would quietly follow

into what they call love. but it had only been days, a mere few since she had told me about the love that hurt her still.

    for a little while there, on that empty street, meera and i were just staring at each other, looking for one expression or another to determine our next move that night. the light from the street lamp falling on us, made it feel like magic, almost.

    "is there something you want to tell me, deb?"

    there was so much, meera. so much that was overwhelming me in that moment, thinking if i was willing to take a leap as long.

    "wanna grab some dessert?"

    "deb?"

    "yeah?"

    "you didn't answer."

    "maybe the star doesn't always need to die, you know."

    "but what if it does?"

    "we keep the light alive inside us."

***

[5]

"you talk about leaving like it's christmas."
"sorry, what?"
meera is laughing. her face faintly visible with the only light in the room coming from the skylight, painting a picture so poignant that i forget what i am saying for a moment and just stare.
she is staring at me too. i lean in and close my eyes. she pulls back.
"weren't you saying something about christmas?"
"so we are playing this game today?"
"which game?"
what follows is meera running around the house with me chasing after her, before both of us are too tired and slump onto the couch. i put my arms around her and she falls over me, our faces now inches apart.
"you really don't believe i would stay, do you?" she asks, her head resting over my chest, hearing my heart grow louder.
"wouldn't be surprising from someone who talks about leaving all the time."
"why do you think i do what i do?"
"we have been over this, haven't we?"

"this isn't about that."

"..."

"you know, there have been so many instances when i have wanted people to stay and unsurprisingly every time i asked them, they said they would."

"so did i, meera. i told you i would stay"

"i know," she says, "but none of the others did."

***

[6]

it is happening again. i am falling in love or maybe not. how can i?

so beautiful, almost lyric-like, watching him sleep. his wavy hair against my face, his hands holding on to thin air with a smile that makes me wonder if he is dreaming. he says he doesn't have dreams, only nightmares that repeat. his breathing is measured, like counting every moment that he is alive, counting every moment that we are together.

i am waiting for him to wake up and tell me things that have quietly grown on me. i used to be afraid of being loved. of becoming the moon. his fingers tip-toeing over my skin, to my face, tracing all that he makes me feel, it doesn't make me run away.

"meera…," he mumbles with eyes half-open. i shut him up with a kiss.

his hands, trembling, hold on to my palms, cold as the heart he had found me with. there is warmth in there, a sense of having lost the emptiness to something whole, something with arms wide open.

there is a tune on my lips, humming to the quietness of this love i do not recognize. of a love that, perhaps, does not recognize me. but here it is, hovering over us like a fragrance from scented incense, suspended in nothingness, this love. unknowing, unaware. waiting.

i know so little about him. madness and melancholy, together, wrapped into one, is what i hear when he speaks to me about how humans make him uncomfortable. "what about me, deb?"

and each time i ask him this, there is only that smile and words that do not make sense to me. words that make me want to believe that i too, can be in love.

***

breathless

[1]

for a while there, back at the cafe, i couldn't help falling in love with meera. all over again. she was dancing to a number i remember from one of our many lifetimes together, asking me to join her. the rest of it is still a blur, almost unwilling to show itself while she and i could swear to anything and everything that was asked of us.

on her lips were words that were too light for the waves to carry. and so i got up, went closer, and asked her to whisper in my ear. she held on to me, her head resting quietly on these shoulders, our bodies moving to what seemed like an unending song about the entirety of us.

"five minutes to twelve," she said, and pulling me to a corner, went down on her knees.

she put out an empty hand and stayed mum.

"meera!"

"..."

"is this because i am..dying?"

"give me your hand."

as i do, she gets up and whispers to me about all the times that we have been apart on new year's eve, in near-perfect detail. of all the times that we wished we were star-crossed lovers that people would write books about. of two people, who, having gone through days of despair, were still willing to stay together.

    a countdown begins inside the cafe.

    meera and i stare at the giant clock and its hands moving along to what is supposedly its greatest moment each year, wondering if this is what love was.

    "maybe not," she says, "but this is enough."

    "this is enough."

***

[2]

not much is said until it is time to say goodbye. we are at the airport, waiting to board two different flights. you walk right by me, with headphones around your neck, carefully hiding the daffodil you decided to get last week. for a moment, i look around. everyone is so oblivious to the obliviousness between us.

    you take a seat the farthest you can from where i am, and while i smile at the absurdity of this love seemingly lost, it just feels like one of those things you do not believe. perhaps, just one of the things that your mind conjures to make it easier. 'the oblivious airport,' i begin to type when i hear someone playing 'kuhad' in the background. there's a tap on my shoulder. a tap so familiar that i wait for it to repeat. once, twice and again, till you are standing right in front of me.

    the smugness almost makes me laugh before i realize how we had been fighting only hours earlier, back at the house which had seen us going through the motions since before this love had begun to set in. maybe it was always there? maybe we would never know.

    "nice to meet you," i say, standing up and putting my hand out.

    "what are you doing here?"

there's that smugness again, that fades away for a moment when i stare at you with no obvious answer. for a while, i wonder what to say, and when there is nothing that comes out, i turn to face the other side.

"deb?"

"yes?" i say, and feel your hands around me. you hold me there like that, now oblivious to the people around us.

"why is it so difficult leaving you behind?"

"you are not leaving anything behind"

"..."

"home will always be right where you leave it, meera"

***

[3]

"you ever wonder why people are so scared of love?"
    "but it's funny though, isn't it?"
    "what is?"
    "the fear of something beautiful?"
    "have you never felt that?"
    "felt what?"
    "that fear of being so much in love with me?"
    she smiles, grabs one of my cold, empty palms inside the blanket, and pulls herself closer.
    "you don't plan to leave, do you?"
    "you know what i am talking about."
    "..."
    "i mean, how can you not be scared of giving someone your love while hoping that they keep it safe?"
    "still funny though."
    faces gazing in different directions, our fingers quietly fiddle.
    "deb?"
    "yes?"
    "do you feel vulnerable?"
    i stay quiet for a few moments.

"i don't see how it is possible to have one and not the other."
"sorry?"
"love and vulnerability."
"maybe that's what love is all about, you know."
"being vulnerable?"
"choosing to be."

***

[4]

late last night, meera woke up in cold sweat again. it has been a couple of months since her father's death.

"why can't we just tell people we love them?" she asked me.
"we can."
"you don't understand. it's not always so easy."

for hours, meera would sit near her father's old chair, staring at it, like it was somehow talking to her. she would sometimes pull me to her side and tell me happy stories from her childhood, all the while vocal about how her father was a different man when her mother was still alive.

"how long would you keep this against him?"
"as long as it takes"
"it's been too long, meera."
"apparently not enough," she would say, and going back to being buried in her work. a couple of weeks after his death, meera had started documenting her father's artwork in her photo journal, making inanimate things that belonged to him look like they were alive.

it was, perhaps, a way of making her feel closer to the person who had quietly pushed her away when she needed him most. she had found writings that he had never mentioned to her, letters that screamed of his inability to love meera the way he wanted to.

"i guess some of us don't even know what it feels like to be home anymore."
"..."
"dad mentioned this in one of his letters."
"meera, you need to stop."
"maybe i was wrong to let him push me away."
"you can do little when the other person doesn't want to let you in."
"didn't you?"
"what?"
"be there?"
at that moment, all i wanted to do was let her hide.
"you know, we keep complaining of how people should love us, but never for once stop to think if we are doing enough."
"what more could you have done?"
"told him that i loved him."
"and that would have made it better?"
"would have made it easier for me to let go."

***

catching

[1]

"what makes you believe in people?"
    "helps to hold on to something."
    "but they always disappoint."
    "not always."
    "always."
    in a way, i agreed with how meera thought about people. almost everyone i had ever held on to had let go, days after saying they wouldn't. but somehow, i still held on to the hope that some wouldn't, that some would stay.
    "i don't think you really do," she says and goes on to click pictures of the street we are in. this old city has always felt like a graveyard of travelers. a place for people to come back to when they were done doing everything they loved.
    meera has a habit of doing this; reading my mind ever so often and avoiding the conversation that would follow.
    "if people didn't disappoint, would you give me a chance?"
    she pretends to not listen and hums to a song that i remember passing on to her playlist on our first morning together. a song whose name i had found scribbled on the back of a discarded love letter. funny the things people throw away, the things you find when you are not looking.

a man passes by and looks at us like we don't belong here. and maybe we don't. so many of us don't but have nowhere else to go.

"it is important to know when to let go," meera declares out loud. a few windows rattle.

"even more important to know when not to."

meera turns back at me for a moment, away from everything else, and smiles.

※※※

[2]

"when it's lost, where does it go?"

"..."

"all this love, when people lose it, where does it go?"

"do you think this..love between us will leave too?"

"not everything i ask is about us."

meera, always the questioning kind. she is reading me a page from her favorite short, our backs against each other, each looking at two ends of this room that would soon be empty. we are moving to a different city.

every letter, being traced by her fingers as she reads them out loud, is carefully floating somewhere my attention is not. i am busy noticing the details of this house that has seen us go through so much together. the first time meera had the courage to say that she wanted to live with me. our first monsoon was spent washing mud off each other's shoes on sundays and mondays were spent trying to wake each other up for tea.

now that we are leaving, it feels like the end of the beginning.

"you are thinking about it again, aren't you?" asks meera, her face now over my shoulders.

"it's just..."

"scary?"

"yeah, i mean, we are moving together but this place has so many things."

"memories," she corrects me and recalls some of her favorites at this house. the very first day we moved in together and how we ended up finding an old notebook in one of the cupboards. a bunch of half-written letters to an unknown somebody by another unknown somebody.

in a way, i think that's what becomes of our stories. forgotten memories, half-written letters, lucky to be found when someone isn't looking. perhaps even making it to another story in an entirely different form.

meera taps on my shoulder. she has a notebook in her hand.

"shall we?"

"become stories for a stranger?"

smiling, i wrap my arms around her.

"it doesn't go anywhere, meera."

"what?"

"this love, when it's lost, why does it need to go anywhere?"

***

[*3*]

this is our time. minutes after midnight, hours before dawn.
    on the terrace, talking in whispers still, our shadows buried somewhere in the dark.
    "you don't need to look so worried all the time," he says.
    i am laughing. the idea of him dying has slowly grown on us. maybe it won't be so terrifying after all.
    "deb?"
    "i know."
    the nights seem so comforting with him around. his fingers tapping the air, playing a song.
    "do you hear it?"
    "..."
    "us, dancing, swaying, moving to this quietness of being."
we belong here. him and i. and perhaps also this love.
    "if it wasn't for my fear of losing you, do you think we'd be here?"
    "does it matter?"

***

[4]

have you ever had this feeling? to sneak out before another chore comes calling. another day turning into another night and before you know it, it's over.

    that's how it felt sometimes. staring at meera, who would be gazing at the sky and the stars.

    she and i had fumbled upon this ritual of stargazing only recently. she said we hadn't made enough memories for her to remember me with. and so here we were, in the middle of nowhere, two people in love, one dying and another waiting.

    "why'd they lie?" she says.

    "about what?"

    "how the moonlight makes your face glow in the dark?"

    she is trying to break this silence, make us forget things that weren't really in our control anymore.

    we went back to staring at those stars she so hoped could keep me alive a little while longer.

    meera is humming now, a billy joel song from the 70s that she keeps asking me to listen to.

    "what if we could stay here?"

    "in the middle of nowhere?"

    "stuck at this moment, right here."

"deb!"
"..."
"it's okay."
and just like that, i hold meera close and begin to cry.

***

falling

[1]

"there is so little to think about when we are together."

i smile. meera and i have spent a year together. we don't know if this is how it's going to stay. but for now, this feels like everything we have wanted. i love how her eyes travel from place to place in a room she is so familiar with, looking for the little changes that she can scribble about in her journal. she says she'd leave it for me to read when she dies. maybe she wants this to stay too.

struggling over a bunch of polaroids from her last trip, she tells me that i don't tell her things. that she is the only one with a backstory in this relationship. i tell her that i don't really have stories to tell about myself.

"what about your parents? would they like me?"

"aren't we getting a little ahead of ourselves?"

with mock anger on her face, she goes back to her struggle with the stolen memories.

"i never really understood their relationship, you know?"

"sorry?"

"i don't remember the last time i saw either of them doing something that felt like love."

meera sits with her head facing down for a moment and then comes closer to me with the album that was half empty still.

"you know what i would really want if we stayed together?"

"that i make breakfast every day?"

laughing, she tells me this story of her parents eloping when they were nineteen.

"i don't think we'd need to elope."

"to keep our hearts close," she says.

"what?"

"i hope we never forget to hold each other close when the days are distant and the nights cold."

***

[2]

for the rest of our lives. we may not live again this moment. i mean. we may never find this moment of unbridled, uninhibited feelings ever again. we have arrived on top of what seems like the end of the world; for you, for me, for all that exists of us. you are laughing. and i? i'm staring at you, my senses having somehow blocked out all noises up here except for the high-pitched frequency of joy.
    of you.
    you and i are on top of the tallest hill the stranger guided us to. the skies are watching over us. the light, somewhere close behind.
    if i died at this place, right now, would they let me stay buried up here, under the mist-covered grass?
    your face is so full of hope, meera. that it makes me believe this is somehow going to make up for all the years we wouldn't be spending together.
    you reach out with your glove-covered palms and come closer to where i am sitting. your arms around me, my face resting on your shoulders. staring at the clouds that don't seem to mind the proximity between us. passing through us almost, oblivious of this tendency to love.
    one of them looks like a leaf, you tell me.

like the one, you asked me to keep? it is inside the notebook that holds a few things i want to leave you with. things i hope you choose to remember on a tuesday afternoon when it rains. i hope it does, you know. rain, i mean.

you look at your watch and ask if i want to leave. the sun probably won't be out anytime soon, you say.

it already is, i want to tell you.

"in a while, meera," i say, "in a while."

***

[3]

on your lips, i find my name.

we are both breathless, gasping from beneath the gaps still left between us. there is little to say, so much for our bodies to know. our skin, dripping with sweat, our hands clasped together, just about.

you say you don't remember the last time someone touched you. you say you have wanted this.

so i take myself down to your breasts, sucking on them gently, as you moan. your moans are not in rhythm as they say. nothing is when two bodies are at each other.

i lift my head to see your eyes closed, and i move further down to your wetness.

you let out a moan, louder this time, and then there is silence. my tongue in places you want it to be, your hands on my head, pushing me in a little deeper.

the surroundings are quiet. or maybe it is just me. i have wanted this too, to be so close that no noise reaches us anymore. moving in circles at first and then in no order at all, it is all chaos, with only this delirious need for animalistic intimacy.

and in a few seconds, the tides have turned, now moving down from over me, as i see you open and close your mouth in childlike ecstasy. my hands on your hips, and us, moving together to this lack of rhythm, to this mayhem we brought upon each other. this mayhem we want not to stop.

    you open your eyes for a few seconds more this time, telling me that it's time we both close our eyes and wait for the closure.

    moments later, i ask if you, too, would leave.

    and on your lips, i find my name.

✳✳✳

[4]

"do you think they would name something on us someday?"

i laugh. meera, in her usual sober stupor, is blabbering on about how she wishes to hear our names being read about in literature. we are where she calls our secret place, our hidden spot in the hills where people are probably too scared to climb down to. it isn't entirely secret, to be fair, but right now, it's just us.

she's always been so fascinated about naming people, and places and placing things in a box. for me, ever since we met that night, i have known not to box this, what we have, into anything at all.

"are you scared?" she asks.

"why'd i be scared?"

there's that smile and the all-knowing look. she is about to say something, but somehow, for some reason, she stops. she pulls out a red dahlia from her pouch and keeps it on my open palm.

"maybe we should leave this here for it to be found by someone."

"meera?"

"i know this is scary, but i promise i am not doing this for you," she says.

somehow it feels like she's lying in a way. i feel i would perhaps do the same if i was on the other side of the boat, to know that the person you have grown to love would soon not be there; it is a monumental ask. to know that they are going to lose and, yet, ask them to hold on with a smile. but in a way, i think we are nothing if not the people that die within us. those that are only supposed to arrive and depart, leaving you with a few empty passports to show.

it is time to leave, i tell her. she asks me to stay for a few more. and so i close my eyes and sit down to listen to these two, beating hearts inside what would probably become something someday. or maybe it wouldn't.

maybe it would just be our dahlia. waiting.

***

[5]

some love stories are meant to be, says meera, with her quintessential poker face on display. seeing my lips twitch, trying hard to maintain the facade of seriousness, she bursts out laughing before i quietly follow. for three years, she keeps reminding me of the time we have known each other. does it not feel longer? i'd have liked to ask. maybe a while later when she is drunk enough to lie.

    i stare at her with a strange sense of detachment still. you know how there are days you can feel as if you are sitting next to a stranger, despite them having seen through all your carefully crafted masquerading? but this isn't the uncomfortable kind that existed before. the kind where we would sit across the bed or in adjacent rooms while she would talk to a stranger she said she had felt a strange connection with. running away from every feeling that she felt could stay for more than a few fleeting seconds.

    but those who have seen us together and apart, meera and i were anything but meant to be, i mean. i don't think people truly realize that the whole must-be-together narrative does not hold true all the time.

    i particularly remember this one conversation from our very early days. we'd talk about clouds that didn't rain and a love that didn't last., and we decided that until we do find that in each other, we'd find ourselves something that doesn't go, something that stays. and sometimes, you gotta have a little faith.

now i am not saying there was any guarantee that we'd end up together. but sometimes, you must be open to going farther than you first hoped to because even though love may eventually be that box of chocolates, you might as well have to wade through the raisin-filled ones before you find what you are looking for.

***

moans

[1]

meera,

    where do we go from here? you and i have come so far along this journey that seemingly started not too long ago to not think about going back. but going forward, with no satisfactory conclusion in sight, i wonder what would happen if i didn't die soon. of course, my likeness to death jokes has clearly gotten better, as you must have noticed through the last couple of months.

    the letter you wrote yesterday made me grin from ear to ear while also bringing up questions i didn't think i would have to think about in the short while that i had been promised. but supposing there wasn't this temporal sword hanging over, i wonder how we would have moved on with this love. the four-letter word that once had us in splits during cinema of excess is now often a blanket of quiet we are too scared to cover us with.

    so much so that it takes words, written and carefully curated, to exclude all that our faces would otherwise not be able to hide. but i am not complaining, only observing how you no longer sleep facing the other side when the memories get pulled over for speeding. have you also noticed how i have begun to share my favorite quilt without too much fuss? but i think it is perhaps also because the nights are now colder than they have ever been.

this may seem like an exaggeration to a cynic who sides with logic more than magic (bloody muggle). still, if you listen closely to the sputtering rain and stare at the windows that scream for help, you will find they are trying to tell us how this love you have come to feel too much of, it has a tune to it – that you can listen to if you keep the heart open for more.

if you are wondering how to stop me from talking in cheap metaphors and instead make me teach you more of those songs that you seem to have built a home out of, you know what to do. stay a while longer in bed on mornings that smell like spring.

deb

***

[2]

crystal clear. i remember the last time meera and i stepped out of the house to buy flowers. it was among the many rituals that had come to be planned by mostly my father, who seemed to have taken a sudden interest in our relationship. it was particularly awkward because i couldn't remember baba bringing a flower for maa. maybe their love was from a different time. i don't know. meera says i don't quite get it, the concept of love.

is there anything to understand? a chemical reaction for those that lean on science, and history for others; i don't know how to define love and put it in a box such that every couple under the winter morning sun agrees. whenever you think this is it, life throws a gentle curveball as a reminder to tell you that there is more. or maybe there is none. a great deal of our often loveless lives is spent trying to figure out if we are even made for something so celebrated by pop culture.

these days, i reminisce upon my memories a fair bit longer. as meera correctly put it in one of her letters, the past sometimes creates enough void inside us that we can go back and fall into, away from perhaps even the flowers that now act like bookmarks inside forgotten books.

her love is a strange thing. sometimes it is there in abundance, so much so that you wonder whether your heart would ever be able to accumulate enough, and yet, there are days when you have to take a step back. when she wants you to reason, and reason hard enough to make this all believable. but how do you make something such as love seem tangible enough to be held in an embrace, or defined in a 100-page novella? she is adamant it is possible, and i just don't know how.

"maybe it is never enough," she says. i place my warm hands on her cheek, and ask her if she would like a dance. she can't stop laughing. you see, i don't know how to. that was one of the many things i made her sign up for when she said she wanted this. but you can't do that in love.

well, maybe i don't understand it well, the concept of love. but i believe you don't have to. you need only fall. the rest is taken care of.

***

[3]

what do you do when it gets too much? when there are enough smiles on the outside for you to breathe in and make balloons out of, if you are still not able to put up your brightest clothes, i wonder if it makes me unlovable. this word, you know, this one word has so often made me feel like a fish outside a bowl. deb often tells me that it doesn't. and his words have enough comfort to crawl into and build a hurt-proof house.

    but here's the thing. i have never really been out of water. even when it seems like the bowl is no longer there, it is because it has quietly been replaced with the sea. and this heart dies faster in unfamiliar surroundings than it perhaps would in a vacuum. take this instance for example. when deb said he could no longer do whatever i thought this was, i should have felt relieved; relieved that he would no longer try to find us love.

    but instead, what i did was pull him back with not promises but what ifs that i thought could forever act like safe deposit boxes i could just put a hand into whenever i wanted and restart. how romantic, he once joked when i told him.

    i don't know what makes this special. the entire going round and round in circles of i love you but do you, before ending up like the shore and the sea. it is almost unbelievable that a person who until a year ago could have picked up a bag full of memories without looking back would be longing for a love that is sitting in front of her, smiling, and writing what is perhaps another letter he thinks i would need when he no longer can.

in a way, this love that i have for deb has also been a way to find that this heart can. that it has the capacity to be a giver without wants, without having to constantly find another picture-perfect heartbreak. that even things you felt had long ceased to exist, on the inside, have a way of coming back.

it's just that, when they do, you must be ready. you must be willing to kiss the sea.

***

[4]

"how often do people lie when they say they are fine?"
"why'd you ask?"
meera and i were back to being our usual, introspective selves after a very long time. death, ironically, had taken a backseat since the lockdown started, and we were forced to bear only each other all day. we weren't complaining; things inside had strangely taken a turn for the better. we no longer talked about letting go, and when we did, it was probably to convince the other for a batch of pav bhaji from last night.
at this point, i didn't know what i feared more; staying in long enough for us to start thinking that it was all going to be alright, or waking up one day to know that i was no longer sleeping beside her. but who was i kidding? i had begun to hope again. no matter how unrealistic, or grounded in fiction it might be, it was hope at the end of the day. and nobody, not even perhaps me, could make it go away.
"the uncle who stays in the adjacent flat, he said he was fine but i don't think he was," she says, staring absentmindedly at a self-help book she'd been pretending to read for months.
i pour two cups of tea for the both of us and move to the other room. i can see her smiling, having stolen a look at what she thinks is the wrong color for chai, but this wasn't

the time for a sarcastic remark; we were too busy dunking our biscuits so they don't fall off and become the little gooey thing that every sane person hates.

"what if i asked you?"

"i'd obviously tell you i'm fine because i am."

"but you are concerned about plenty of things, aren't you? let's see if we begin to list them…"

"no, no, that's not the point, and i know what you are doing here."

a few light punches later, we sit down panting, clearly tired of a conversation that didn't go anywhere except perhaps her journal and one of my letters. i find it rather strange how more people do not recognize these silent evenings spent doing nothing. when did love become about everyday butterflies?

"all i'm saying, meera, is that people need to lie to themselves sometimes."

"and that's okay?"

"maybe, maybe not, but who are you and i to decide?"

**

[5]

gentle. soft. tender. the only words that one would perhaps associate with this person who fell asleep while trying to keep staring at me. what do i do with this love? this infinite seeming love that deb tells me he has for me, i am still trying to figure out a shelf to keep it, or maybe i would end up needing an entire trophy cabinet.

but is that what i must do? keep his love, not in a photograph he made me click for what he calls our happy album, but as a trophy to look back at and continue reminding myself that there exists this person i can always fall back upon? you see, it is hard for me to give it all up, this carefully built barrier, to start believing in a person even if they show you the world you have always wanted to live in. going down that loop again is a big no-no.

you don't fall for the same thing over and over again. not if you are sane enough. i have been through the love that encompasses all else and the one thing i am certain about is the apparent lack of it just when you are all in. it's almost like a hide-and-seek game where you are blindsided by their absence before you realize that it is, in fact, permanent.

have you had someone come to tell you that everything you do makes perfect sense even if in your mind nothing does? to be seen bare, with your heart wrapped in a winter blanket, that is what deb does to me every time we talk, and i go quiet during our conversations. fitting long-lost pieces into the jigsaw puzzle and making me realize that i could still be whole again after all this time. that i do not need to keep things as they are, and there's a possibility, however remote, that i would see the sunset again without thinking about maa.

he is jolted out of his slumber with an 11 o'clock alarm that he set so that i have something before i sleep. staring at me while still in his usual child-like stupor, he blinks his eyes twice and points to the refrigerator. "there's some caramel pudding, don't forget i have another alarm to remind you," he says and goes back to sleep.

and me? i will wait for him to remind me again.

***

louder

[1]

meera. meera. meera.
    does it sound strange to you? it does to me. on many nights, i stay awake long after meera has fallen asleep beside me, only to be able to see her. when it's quiet.
    so quiet that the lizards come out in search of their midnight snack, and the only audible sound is that of the hideous polka-dot clock ticking. but that's not strange. i know meera does it too–staying awake to see me asleep. i pretend on most nights.
    what is strange is that i keep muttering that name when i stare at her, as if the woman i love would have her soul come out and tell me things that she wouldn't otherwise. over and over again, muttering a word like counting beads on a rosary, i stare until my eyes give up and the heart decides to take a walk into the night.
    on some days, i don't know whether or not i deserve this love that has come my way. all i know is that it is going to stay. there's no fear of abandonment. no fear of having her leave, for i know her fears far outnumber mine. of how much longer i might have, and holding on to the hope that it wouldn't be as soon as they diagnosed it would be.

mornings to evenings, when neither of us is too excited about work, we take turns to leave each other longing for more like a teenage love that has only blossomed, a little late, but as it has come with more than either of us could hope. waves after waves, washing us over, and yet, never quite enough for this longing that stays.

she doesn't laugh anymore when i tell her these things. no more the oh-so-romantic taunts that would earlier come my way. she just smiles and quietly takes notes that she never lets me see. says she will when it is time and i hope that the time never arrives.

***

[2]

meera,
    like the rain in the summers, or the scorching heat of the winters, some people too are transient. to be fair, all people are but some are more transient than others. unless of course one is dreaming. it does feel like a dream sometimes.
    talking in riddles again, aren't i? you mustn't worry. i have needed this time by myself for a while. if something happens, farhan bhai has promised to call you first. if you feel like throwing that expensive phone at me, think about all the little kids who are struggling to find a morsel of food.
    there, there. that smile is what i was talking about. *kabhi kabhi mann karta hai tumhe kahin na jaane dun, aur sirf dekhta rahun.* but what good would it do to the ache that exists in this heart? i haven't felt this void since the last time you went away. this time, i do not know. seeing so many deaths around us could be a reason. funny how the narrative has shifted from my untimely, unfortunate demise to those of millions.
    life has a cruel sense of humor, and you call me morose!
    i keep seeing your instagram posts from a secret account (no, you are not getting the username). the fact that you have gone back to your love for photography gives me so much comfort. you should consider sending me a postcard with one

of your favorites sometime. i might just make it back sooner in that case.

keep giving weekly updates to maa, please. she'd be worried but she will understand. attached alongside you will find a dried daisy, one that you should keep in the box you stored the leaf.

intezaar mat karna. chittiyan bhejta rahunga.

***

[3]

meera,

    for far too long, we spent our days trying to fill gaps that no longer needed filling. for far too long, we didn't quite realize that this feeling wasn't an existing void, but the fear of creating a new one.

    you and i had known this for a while. spending weeks without talking to each other because what if this too wasn't meant to last, all while thinking of the good times. really though, what were we really doing? every time i asked, you said the reason you wouldn't consider something with me was that i didn't seem like the kind that would leave. you should really have left the humor to me, you see. nevertheless, look at how far we seem to have come because one of us was wise enough to say things out loud.

    alright, we were both not wise. *pata toh hai tumhe, hum dono kitna ganda mazaak karte hain.* you know, that conversation with your dad really helped me see things in a better light. you needed me to be there for a while, and that was enough. sometimes, that's probably all there is to love. we don't always need the missing piece; contentment with the existing jigsaw is sometimes the best you can do for yourself.

now, what more may i say that hasn't already been said? what the spoken and the written words have not yet communicated, is there perhaps a way of showing it in the language of touch?

jaldi milenge, phir batana.

yours

***

[4]

how do you define a longing that only ends with the fingertips of your lover on your lips?

    in words no less. for, the last time they came close to your vicinity was long before you had known what distance meant and the dialing of digits on your cellphone was not enough. his fingers, cold from the shower, meet my arms and then my shoulders.

    the gentleness is innate, meaning he couldn't hurt me even if he wanted to. not that it mattered. i wasn't going to be gentle. i wasn't going to let him. his fingers move from the shoulders to my bare back, replaced now by lips that seem to have missed me. the language isn't silence, but moans that slowly gather pace as we push each other until my back is touching the wall.

    my fingers, meanwhile, have made their way inside to find hardness. the unbearable longing that exists here right now could make me want to do it right there, but the softness of those lips on my neck? they are keeping me busy. it doesn't take long for his mouth to find another and drown down the moans in the room so we only hear beating hearts.

    not a minute longer, he says, and the two bodies that had until now been out of sync pace together to undress and let each other roll on the bed, fighting to take charge until i win.

pinned against the stainless white sheets, he stares at me for a minute before closing his eyes. my mouth kissing his nipples first, before moving down, ever so slowly to the burning loins. foreskin down, my tongue swirling around. up and down, while his head arches back. right when his hands move to my head, i climb over and there's the moan again.

plural now, no longer singular in their frequencies as we inch closer to realizing the longing. his palms on my breasts, as the movements gain momentum. stroke after stroke, moan after moan. his mouth opens and closes, until it opens again and my hands clench his skin.

oh, how i have missed deb.

**

stop

[1]

deb,

    i have seen them go, seen them come, and make the same mistakes over and over, before realizing that this is but a futile attempt at finding love where there exists none.

    the first time we met, when you told me that you wanted the same thing that i did out that night, it was hard for me to believe you. perhaps because of those eyes that find it hard to hide anything at all. and no matter the words that were said, and those that weren't, it felt like a mistake because i wasn't ready for love. to give so much and expect so much more out of another person, i could not find it in me after namit.

    it wasn't his fault at all, you see, he did all that his heart allowed him to, and though i may blame him for leaving when he did, i would probably have done the same thing. the same thing that i expected you to do when it got unbearable to live with a person who couldn't live with herself, and on days when the distance between adjacent rooms must have felt like amsterdam and agra all over again, i almost hoped you'd leave.

    why am i writing this to you on a perfectly rainy day, when things are better and our love no longer needs an anchor? to be fair, i don't know. you said you'd never ask for an explanation. and it scares me still. to think that such love is possible; to understand someone without expectations, and stay while they give you every possible reason to leave, is scary.

but more than anything else, it can make you realize how toxic you can be as a person. to have stayed with a person like me, i wouldn't recommend it to anybody. and i wish i could make it right with namit. and you. so once i am done typing this one, i am going to have to sit down and write one to him as well.

to close a chapter, and hopefully, begin another one. *woh kya kehte the tum? baarishon mein jo aasu dikhe, unhe puchna khush rehne ka raaz.*

i think i have my answer now.

meera

***

[2]

meera,
   there is this strange silence between us. i can't seem to pinpoint the reason, but do you think we are falling apart?
   despite being in the same house, it feels like we are a few continents apart, seeing each other when one of us needs to fill this growing void with touches that have begun to feel forced and unfamiliar. forgive me, but if there was such a thing as the forever you told me about when you inked my name on your skin despite my honest unease, i don't think this is what it is supposed to feel like.
   like missing a flight, over and over, for you just can't seem to wake up from a make-believe dream you thought was how love is supposed to be. but what is really the harm in dreaming about staying together when there is love, belief, and a little bit of fairy dust?
   i know what you are thinking. this letter doesn't sound like the person that you have always known me as; quiet, pragmatic, and never the one to use two when one word would suffice. and you are right, it is not the familiar face you see every day writing this, it is someone who is scared to lose what he didn't know could ever go away. you know, the entire idea of comfort you don't have to worry about? i

have realized how much it can take from the other person in the equation. hearts, fragile hearts, and not pulleys, like you keep saying.

    but at the end of the day, it is about two hearts who have to decide whether or not the love is worth fighting for. i call it a fight because it has felt that way for a while now. we could keep trying newer ways to entertain ourselves, perhaps ones that would end up tearing us apart sometimes, but is that how we want to remember each other?

    or do we want to be the dahlia and daisy kept hidden in a book, until it is alright to open it again and not cry? i hope you decide soon.

    from across the room,

namit

✳✳✳

[3]

namit,

was it really so easy? to let go of me? we got so far; and if i was to be honest, we got far enough for us to go all the way. what i cannot seem to understand, then, is the manner in which things ended. why did they need to when you always said we'd figure it all out together? what'd i do to this stupid tattoo you never asked me to get made?

the things i'm still willing to do to have you back scare me.

but you are not coming back. the phone call last night made sure i didn't go around claiming i was some heartbroken woman who had been left stranded in the middle of a low by her partner. not that, i didn't think of it in the last few days. sleep around a little, and ensure i wallow in self-pity so much that they don't get attached.

the point of this now overlong letter, however, is that i want to tell you things that i can't seem to over a phone call. i'm a little tipsy, can you tell? i'm imagining us. sitting across two ends of a room, our thoughts floating through the low frequencies of our fragile hearts because we are far too distant. this is where you say, "too much information," and we laugh.

but really, what if we were fighting a little more? i don't see that as reason enough to break it off. when did this happen, love, and why could i not see it coming? we deserved a longer conversation. we deserved to have a happy ending. i don't have another person to remind me of the missed visits to maa's grave. wait, did you think i had become too dependent?

alright, alright, i will stop now. you know how thick we go, wine and i. but if i had become so dependent, wasn't it more of a reason to stay?

i hope we don't talk again.

meera

***

[4]

you can only do so much, say whatever comes out, till you inevitably face the one truth you refuse to accept. that it is over. namit and i have been over for a while but his letter was unexpected. unexpected in that i always thought we were going to be the ones other couples talk about when they talk about relationships. but what do people really talk about when they talk about love?

that everything – the butterflies and the ugly you persevered through for it was love – was building up to a giant ball of heartbreak. or do they only talk about the happy days when namit was still calling me at odd hours during the day to check up on me? he stopped doing that a while ago. he thought i was pulling away. i merely needed some time, and i thought he'd understand.

funny the things you expect of people. the entire going blind in love philosophy never made sense to me, until yesterday night at three, when i woke up cold, in a pool of my own sweat. no, love doesn't make you blind to falling for just about anyone. what it really does is it pulls you in, and bides its time till you put all your faith in one place.

i have needed help for a while to deal with what i have long refused to do, and when i thought it was time to tell namit that i needed him there, he decided it was time. maybe it was. trauma has a strange sense of timing, in that it really does not. it manifests as it intends to, no warning bells rung, and leaves little space for help.

as it turns out, seeking help can go a long way as namit told me when he came home last week to take his belongings, things got worse because i stopped talking. and perhaps, he is right in his own way. but why did he never ask? maybe the silence got too comforting.

***

again

[1]

meera,

one of the perks of having a cheesy boyfriend is you get cheesy letters. now i know what you are thinking. why did i not give you these while i was still alive to see your face light up? we shall come to that.

pehle batao, kaisi ho? i hope the sympathizers are treating you well.

okay, sorry. that was probably lame. but you know you miss this. do you also miss having me by your side while falling asleep to our favorite song?

yesterday, i was going through your dad's photo albums when a few letters fell out. they were written by a young couple, still unaware of what the future held, probably even of the fact that they'd someday decide to live together.

is it not strange, though? why can't life be a little predictable; maybe just enough for people to love a little more?

maybe they wouldn't. but while reading those letters, i realized how the things we often consider too small to be asked in a typical conversation would have made so much difference if two people haven't heard each other in weeks.

maybe a smaller world is not as comforting as they promised it would be.

and that's why these letters exist, meera. to provide the comfort i know you would need, even if for a few days after i am gone. to be the paash-baalish to your sleeplessness. when i become a memory for the rest, i hope these letters bring to you a part of everything you loved me for.

when the weight is too heavy, remember to read through these conversations i wish we had the time to have.

don't forget to eat on time.

yours

***

[2]

meera,

it's not about the things we say, is it? the ones said aloud when the walls are watching, wide awake. when we see each other smiling, awkwardly still, because we must.

it's about the ones that make their way to our curled-up toes during winters spent under the dirty razai. carefully tucked under the lie of forever, because these hearts, these tender, fragile hearts have been broken too many times to handle the impossibility of an always.

the day you lost your father and a friend, i remember you smiling when we got home. baba would be happy, you said. and when i got you your chai the next morning, it was like the day before never existed. i never quite figured out why you talked about your mother dying the way you did. but after your dad, i think i have begun to understand.

it does not quite hit you in the beginning at all, does it? you don't operate like me, or the rest of us, crying your heart out at the thought of seeing someone you love getting buried. you do not.

you tuck it inside till you can't.

and then the flux happens. not slowly, but all at once. in the middle of a photoshoot. when you want to relate all your pictures to something that reminds you of the person. and when you can't, you sit down and cry. i wouldn't know what that feels like.

but you can always keep one of these around for when it happens. it would probably not stop the tears, but maybe it is just enough to stop you from seeming like a lunatic. *cue awkward laughter.*

what i am really trying to tell you here, meera, is that it's okay to process things differently. to process grief in ways your heart wants to. if you don't want to talk about it immediately, it's okay. i'd ask the therapist friend to call you every once in a while.

tab tak, let's just hope my death jokes keep you entertained.

yours

***

[3]

meera,

been a while, hasn't it? something tells me you've been waiting since the last one. i'm pretty darn good at cliffhangers, you'd know that better than most people.

enough about inconsequential things. let us talk about something we must; something we should have talked about a long time ago: happiness. a concept so strange that it has kept us, you and i, up on nights that were spent measuring distance and the remaining minutes of the international calling plan. when you were in amsterdam, trying hard not to come back to what you called a potential disaster waiting to happen, you said you didn't know what it meant.

to be happy, you said, was something that only existed in my words and your photographs. and maybe you were right. we often search for things we crave in things that are unreal. i don't quite know what we hope to find. when we look for something so exceptionally real in people we carefully curate it to suit our immediate needs, i wonder if it is even fair to the other person who perhaps has no clue about these unreasonable expectations.

but love, tell me, what did you feel the first time you heard me sing for you? hey, no, not the obvious feeling of wanting to choke my neck so i never do something so blasphemous as singing a tagore again. i am talking about the unusual smile that followed when you googled up the meaning. or if you wish to go further back, remember the nights spent under the moonlit blanket of blue, listening to nothing but each other's breath.

you see, those moments, when you think about them, hear the crashing waves and a few butterflies fluttering still, those were times happiness knocked on the door for a little while. and while it may have soon left because it's got to be with somebody else, like an estranged lover, know that it would be back. unlike people.

and so hold on to them you must, for that is what you'd need before you have some new ones.

yours

***

[4]

he's been writing something these past few days. says i would know when i need to.

how much more time i wonder. that we'd have to live with this fear of not being by each other's side one morning. him, someplace better, and i, holding on to whatever remains of him. a few memories, perhaps a few notes of love that he keeps hidden inside my dad's photo album.

sometimes i ask myself: why? why would i need to go through the motions of never wanting to love someone to loving someone so much that i do not know what to do once this is gone? having everything one moment to losing everything you hold dear, i've forgotten how it feels.

life has a strange way of bringing things back to you. like the sea.

washed so far away that you start feeling that something doesn't exist. and just when this heart is busy believing this lie, the waves, the tides bring it back to you. memories of a lost night, washed ashore, without a warning.

like it wants you to remember the hurt that came, and this time, not push it back somewhere but feel what you must. to know what it's like to see them wither in front of your eyes.

"meera?" he says, while i wrap myself closer to his warmth under the blanket.

"thought you were asleep."

"what are you thinking about?"

"what do you think?"

he doesn't say much, deb. just as quietly, he holds my palm and nestles himself under me.

"i think this is better."

***

[*5*]

deb,

    these last few days, i love that you have been teaching me tagore. although you call yourself a hapless romantic, it seems almost strange how little i have heard you humming to these songs before the lockdown put us together far longer than either of us had hoped. and it surprises me still how little i know about the man who promises to love me till he dies.

    you close your eyes every time you listen to some song your mom used like a lullaby. and you smile, as if seeing yourself relive those moments over and over, squeezing the last little bit that time has let us have. as for me, i do not know whether to be happy that you are happy with the acceptance that has quietly washed us all over, or to be watchful that you don't go away too soon.

    even when we are both laughing, sometimes at your naivete when it comes to humor, it feels like there is a certain void that has us in a tight embrace so we don't go overboard with happiness.

    consider this a letter that says everything that remains unsaid. but is it fair to say that i will miss these times of having to stay locked up with you? don't get your hopes too high. okay, i know you have the all-knowing look spread across your face as you read that last line. but i swear i won't miss this at all. except perhaps for the sex, i don't think i would miss much.

alright, maybe i would miss eating what you make after spending hours on youtube, and maybe, i would miss the conversations that follow every time you introduce me to a new song. but your incessant need to tell me how you love me, and expect me to go along; you don't really expect me to miss the cringe too, do you?

where am i going with this? i don't know, love. i feel the love that you so often write about in your so-so after-letters. and it is too much. this overwhelming feeling of longing for someone who is right in front of you, is there a drug for this malady? i hope not to find any answers, deb, only have enough time to have these questions come up more often.

until then, i will cringe at your failed attempts at romance while you teach me songs that talk of the full moon on a lonely summer night.

meera

***

silence

[1]

"why do you always write about sad things?"
"what'd you have me write about instead?"
"i don't know, maybe about how happy i make you."
while we both laugh, she goes on to click photos of this new cat in our neighborhood, i wonder if this is the same girl who had once been so averse to the idea of love that she'd refuse to even talk about other couples. while i won't call myself much of a romantic either, seeing meera say the things she says, and do the things she does still comes as a surprise.
from making love on a sultry sunday afternoon to hitching a ride to the nearest metro, there isn't an activity where she doesn't stop to talk about love. sometimes through humor, sometimes through her eyes; it's an ephemeral thing now, much like the letters i'd send. always existing, seen, and felt by only the two people that it is meant for.
"would you love me always?"
"in sickness and in health."
"you are just doing it for the sex."
"maybe! am i?"
her gentle punches on my arm are followed by sloppy kisses and fumbling fingers. our skins melt onto each other,

into a potpourri that smells a lot like promises. not to be found by those seeking but finding those who seek hope. i believe that's what we are searching for, too, almost every day when we wake up with our hands tightly knit.

people in love are so often carried away by what cannot be, that they refuse to see what can. meera and i could have so easily been thrown apart. at one point, i thought we were destined to. holding on was a matter of chance or maybe not. certainly not.

destiny can only do so much if you ask me. for, i would choose meera every single time. remember what hassan said? for you, a thousand times over. because what is love if not choose them, over and over, every single time that you have to make a choice?

***

[2]

meera,

"*tumhe film music isliye pasand hai kyunki woh aasan hai?*"

like aisha in wake up sid, *kabhi kabhi tum bhi aisi kuch cheezein keh deti ho* that makes me sit back and smile. your maturity often takes centre stage when talking about things such as relationships, but when i see you at any other time, it is hard to believe that you are the same person.

this dichotomy in you is strange and lovable on equal levels. how? don't ask me. if only i could find an answer for why i stuck around for so long after being asked to leave a few hundred times. i know that was a low blow, but you owe me that much, don't you think? *aur main nahi kahunga toh kaun kahega?*

Cheesy but there's only so many days i can go without cheese, sex, and you, and it has really been too long since i got either of them. you see, the old caretaker here has 12 kids, and i got sad thinking we don't even have one to show for all the wild things we do in bed. i agree my humor really hasn't improved all these years.

there's also a little surprise attached to this letter, as you'd have noticed. follow the map, and you should be able to find me. not that i want you to, but i wouldn't want you to miss out on the most amazing momos and the finest cuddles in the multiverse. not so selfish after all. alright, a little bit, but a dying man deserves a little leeway.

sad ho gayi? bas phir aa jao. barf bhi hai, dopamine bhi. without you, it's been a little tough getting sleep at night. might just be the mosquitoes but maa said something about a quote from gulzar sahab last week and thought i should send it to you: *"tere jaane se toh kuch badla nahi. raat bhi aayi thi, aur chaand bhi tha. haan magar neend nahi."*

intezaar rahega. for your letter, and for you.

yours

***

[3]

dear deb,

i know what you'd be thinking: what's with the dear? but hear me out: the easiest way to catch someone's attention, especially when they are upset about something you did, is to do what you don't. now imagine me playing badshah the next time we make love or fuck. well, this is cheating. but you know what they say about love and war. this isn't war, of course, not even close.

kabhi kabhi mere dil mein khayal aata hai, what would we be if not star-crossed lovers destined to meet in the unlikeliest of circumstances, only to fall in love when one is about to die? it is probably not as dramatic as i am making it sound, but you always said i have a thing for theatrics, and this is as good a time to show you all the crazy parts of me.

don't you worry, though; i will make it up to you this time, just like i always do. don't shake that stupid head of yours; i do make it up to you in my own little ways; you just don't know it yet. i don't let the people i love know.

except, of course, when there's a fight where i am the perpetrator, and since i am me, who doesn't know how to console people after upsetting them, i do the next best thing. crack silly jokes or give them a literal saccharine overdose. my therapist says it's unhealthy, but how does it really matter as long as my boyfriend is smiling as widely as he is right now?

sadness doesn't look good on you, love. and while i can only hope it goes away soon, i promise to do better like i always do. there's not enough my heart can muster for all that you do to keep up with my whims and fancies, and yet loving me like you did the first time we met, but it isn't a lie when i tell you about this love i have and would continue to. it isn't a lie when i tell you that you are my happy place.

forever yours,

meera

***

[4]

meera,
jaag rahi ho? haan, jaag toh rahi hi ho.
is this a letter? an extended text message? or is this a checklist of unfinished sentences during our conversations that don't seem to end even after we have talked into the wee hours of the morning?
honest answer: i don't know. strange, considering how i pretend to have all the answers. but stranger things happen, such as when people are scared of a special something in the present because of a past that is now a tangled ball of once-comforting wool.
pata hai, meera, i notice words. even the ones you don't say out loud.
and i want to say so much. but having known bits of you through the little time we have had together, i don't want to scare you as someone in a rush. you see, i don't see this as a speeding car in a sprint. no, i'd rather we be the proverbial turtle, walking through a beach with only pit stops on the way.
pardon the excessive use of clichés, and i tend to go overboard in love.

sau baat ki ek baat hai, ki tum mujhe pasand ho. kis tarah se, kyun, aur yahan se kya; all of this for later. for now, all that matters is that you know. in this life, there are going to be so many obstacles, and i know that you know, but i, for one, like it when people reassure me with nothing but words.

so when i tell you things are going to be fine, trust that we will work on it together.

kaafi kuch likhna baaki hai. kaafi kuch kehna bhi. bas, itna kahunga ki, koshish karte jaana hai. baaton baaton mein pal beet jaana hai.

for you to keep safe.

✲✲✲

[5]

deb,

tumhara khat mila.

imagining the cringe on your face while reading is enough reward for me. but no, seriously, how cheesy can you get? you did actually say a few pretty interesting things in that email but let's not get too ahead of ourselves here. you are you, and i am me because this is what this is. maybe in a different world, we would live happily ever after.

i know, i know. you hate those two little words enough to file a plea to have them removed, but an 'almost there' is better than a 'never again' in my book. it is better than being promised a forever that leaves you waiting. to live through a maybe is easier than the two extremes you believe in.

on a less serious note, though, i was thinking about something last night. what would happen if a curious postman decided to read a letter sent from one long-distance lover to another and found full-blown erotica inside? no - that doesn't imply i want one from you (not that i would mind in any case), but it's been a while, you see.

you were expecting a little more right there, weren't you? don't shake that bobble-like head of yours; you romantics are what is infesting this world, you know. if it weren't for people like you, i would be chilling with a white beer in one hand and grapes in another, with a sugar daddy who didn't ask me for love. but here we are, no thanks to you.

lekin ek baat bataun? kabhi kabhi dar lagta hai. kya hoga jab tumhe samajh aayega ki mujhe pyaar karna hi nahi hai.

i know what you keep saying, but hear me out: you can't cure an ailment that isn't one; you can't keep trying to help me with my grief because i don't want this to go away. understand what you will, but at this point, and after so long, this is what i want my life to be like, even if it means never having to hope again.

see me soon.

meera

✳✳✳

goosebumps

[1]

"let's kill each other," she says, and strangely, i am not surprised. if anything, it makes me curious to the extent that i ask her how she wants it to be. she is aware. she smiles sheepishly and snuggles up close to me, brushing her nose against my cheeks. "you are the strangest of men i have known," she says.

i think sometimes she said these things to see if i frowned, and any sane person probably would have, but when i didn't, which was always, she would sit down in a corner and cry. i never asked why. i felt she didn't want me to.

on days when we were dead, meera and i would slip out of our pyjamas with fake life certificates and escape the morgue. we would simply stare at the sky and sleep through the night in silence. some nights she would hum a tune i would tell her i have heard in dreams, and she would tell me that she sneaked into them sometimes. "but i never saw you," i would counter, only to hear her laugh at the absurdity of all that she made me go through, realizing perhaps that love was becoming a part of it.

sometimes, we would phase through the old records store in manhattan, and make ourselves a mixtape of all songs we hated when we were alive, slipping in a couple of cassettes for another time.

in the morgue, too, she would come to the section of natural causes to see me when nobody was watching. "i came to fix your heart," she would joke, and we would break into fits of suppressed giggles, careful not to wake the rest to life. she had thought about that as well, and it had taken me some time to make her realize that not everyone wanted to.

on days when we were alive, we would be too busy. passing by each other on roads not-so-empty with sounds we only fleetingly noticed, meera and i would glance sideways before remembering a phone call we forgot to make. she would come home when i would already be in deep sleep and play the violin, hoping that her lullaby would pull me out of it.

"don't you want to know? don't you want to know why we should kill each other?" she asks.

"so that this love never dies?"

***

[*2*]

"but what about days when i don't feel like loving you?" meera asks.

"then you don't."

"does it work that way?"

"you see all these people, meera? these not-too-different kinds of people who seem too disinterested in crazy, stupid love?"

"hmm."

"what makes you think that they have never experienced love like you and me? their faces, their hearts, or the lines on their palm? what is it?"

i see her staring at me, lost in thought.

"i-i don't know?" she says.

"exactly, meera. you can't. none of us can because that's who we are. incapable of a love that happens every moment, flawed at places you wish we weren't."

"so what can one do?"

"love when you can. and love them well."

***

[3]

you wake up, follow the footsteps of your favorite song, and arrive at your farewell party. you see them all, those that matter anyway, standing there to bid you goodbye. after a while, everyone is making their speeches and you sit, holding hands with the person who makes you want to hold on to life for a few moments more.

that's how death must come. for you. we have had longer than promised, and these last few months have brought with them a sense of quiet to my life. maybe it is the thought at the back of my head of hoarding enough love to last a lifetime. i know that isn't going to happen. i would probably end up moving on too. death is but for the person that goes. for those that remain, what it does is create a constant need to fill empty spaces.

spaces that need love. once you go, i believe i am going to have a few of those. some a reminder, necessary if i might say, of could-have-been. but no, i do not want to make it about myself. in your absence, i must remember the things that made you the person i have come to love. in death, we must remember them for the things they brought to the lives of people they touched and the trail of sunshine left on the blue skyline.

on the skyline painted red during the wee hours of one of our sundays, i shall remember how your face looked with the light falling upon you. glowing, just enough for me to try and capture. or the nights spent in silence at the beach. you know, i might just go back there every time i miss sitting in the cahoot of your words. lafz, like you like to call them.

how much more time must i have to be able to love you enough? i do not know. i'm afraid of watching you leave without saying what you want, without hearing what i want to say. love does not die, you say, but people do. how i wish sometimes you would lie.

***

cuddles

[1]

deb
coming home?
meera
worried about me being with another guy?
deb
yeah yeah whatever.
deb
come soon.
deb
have made butter chicken.
meera
again?
deb
and gajar ka halwa.
deb
again!
meera
what do i do with this love?
deb
eat it, maybe.
meera
you should stop cracking jokes.

deb
this wasn't a joke, this was me sulking.
meera
what is this behavior?
deb
a dying man gets to sulk sometimes, no?
meera
again?
deb
alright, alright.
deb
meera?
meera
deb?
deb
:)
meera:
so cheesy!
meera
just like you cooking the same thing you did two days ago again.
meera
because i wasn't around then.
deb
i was just kidding.
deb
so you come sooner.
meera
really? :(
deb
no.
deb
now don't make sad faces.

meera
:(
deb:
kai raat ki biryani bhi baaki hai
meera
open the door.
deb
what?
meera
your meera is here.
:)

***

[2]

on a friday night, what do you most look forward to?

a dinner date, a trip to the nearest hill station, or if you are a beach person, perhaps a bunch of pina coladas while listening to live music and the cacophonous beats of the sea? perhaps even add a dash of slow dancing if the rest falls short.

for meera and me, fridays are reserved for something else: cooking. not cooking romance, no, we believe i have enough of that for the both of us. throughout the week, and it has increasingly come to feel like a ritual, we send each other youtube videos of things we'd like to cook over the weekend.

and after a bout of drunk sex late on friday, as we wake up with beautiful hangovers the next morning, this lovable ritual starts.

her leg pushes me to get up from the bed and cook us some brunch, and then fall asleep once more until it is time to hit snooze once again. showering the other with sloppy kisses until they are forced to make a face and wake up. playing a badshah song loud enough for the neighbors to start worrying.

but it isn't much about the food as it is the process that makes us look forward to it. her holding me from the back while i chop some carrots for the halwa or stealing kisses while the cats outside look on.

    she laughs every time i smell something i am making, and when asked, she laughs a little more.

***

[3]

deb,

how much longer must i wait to kiss you? it doesn't help that my boyfriend has been spending more time with his female colleagues than doing the work he is supposed to! sometimes i feel like you take these trips to get away from my sometimes annoying need to be around you all the time.

look what you've done! i sound like you, and this is someone who cringed at the thought of love until about a year ago. anyway, the point of this pointless little letter is that i miss you, and if you don't come back soon, i am going to send that impending text to namit.

the fact that you are laughing right now makes me want to punch you.

alright, i am going to behave myself and start misbehaving as soon as you come back. wouldn't i make a superb b-grade movie writer? i even surprise myself sometimes. really though: at this point, there is nothing i wouldn't do for you to keep this from going anywhere.

unlike you, who loves cooking, you know what i most look forward to during weekends? it is time we spend doing the dishes, listening to you talking about your week at work, and humming to the latest old hindi film song you are obsessed with.

how did someone who hated cooking because she hated doing the dishes get here? as you keep saying to whoever will listen, love makes you do the strangest of things without raising any questions or concerns.

aaj ke liye bas itna hi. baaki ka drama for when we meet.
tumhari,

meera

***

[4]

"if you are what you eat, what if i ate clouds?"
"why are you always thinking about food, and why do you sound like me?"
"they say people start sounding like each other if they live together."
"you just made that up."
"all words are made up."
"did you just?"
"yes."
"did you just quote a comic book character?"
"don't push it."
"if my memory serves me right, didn't someone hate superhero movies?"
"focus on the clouds."
"i would much rather focus on you."
"you have started stealing my lines too!"
"meera?"
"deb?"
"shall we?"
"aren't we?"
"you know what i mean."
"i do."

"so?"
"so?"
"it's okay if you don't want to."
"is this a proposal?"
"what if it is?"
"then it is a pretty shoddy effort."
"if i went down on my knees and sang jaane tu ya jaane na, would that suffice?"
"with a diamond ring, it just might."
"you are becoming a little too predictable."
"sorry?"
"did you think i was joking?"
"but…"
"this is it, the end of our infinity saga and hopefully the beginning of many more?"
"but.."
"my knees hurt, now please say yes."
"it's always been a yes."
"not always."
"don't ruin the moment!"
"oh, i am ruining the moment?"
"shut up."
"but…"
"ssshh…"

***

[5]

"hope gave me a little cactus"

what do you make of this line? staying with meera means listening to lines like these almost every day. in trying to understand her during phases like these, where conversations would go nowhere, i have ended up with a diary of little things that i plan to gift on her next birthday.

consider this line for example: i feel like all the water in my body is getting replaced by dust.

what do you make of it?

someone in pain, someone so deep in thought that they have lost all sense of reality?

not meera. five minutes after she said this, she said she loved me for the very first time. you could see it differently, too, of course. that she thinks about me, us, and this relationship only when she feels all hope is lost. but i don't see that as a bad thing.

in fact, it takes me back to one of my favorite lines in all of cinema. where celine tells jesse: "isn't everything we do in life a way to be loved a little more?"

and if you are the first thing that someone thinks of in their time of despair, it can only mean that they expect you to help them feel better. i'd think it is a privilege to be that someone to somebody.

or, in meera's own words: the stars kept falling, and we kept wishing.

***

[6]

isn't *shaam ho chuki hai* such a comforting line?

her eyelashes are doing a dance on my face as she is struggling to open her eyes to the streetlight coming in through the window, and instead of asking me to pull back the curtains, she kisses me, ever so gently, with her chapped lips.

when my hands move inside her oversized white shirt and caress her back, her lips turn into a smile on mine. she goes back to resting her face on my shoulders, eyes still closed and our fingers still tightly clasped.

does she truly love me?

or is it just the comfort at this point? i wouldn't really mind the latter as long as she stays. it is probably a little selfish of me to feel this way, but what would i do without meera?

this is perhaps just me overthinking anyway. if she comes to know, she is going to run me around the house with a belt. before, of course, i make a bdsm joke and we sit down to take a breather from the laughs.

...

for love to be love, what are the parameters?

i can feel his eyes on me. and also this annoying little streetlight coming in through the curtains, but without it, it would be too dark for me to see him. it's a blur, to be honest, but it is his constant need to stare at me while i sleep, that makes this so beautiful.

when our lips collide into a mess, and his hands do what they do best, i can't help but smile at this constant hurry that he has.

but there's no universe where i want anything otherwise.

these moments, this time, and all the love that this man gives me.

i don't know what i have done to deserve it, and i don't know why he stayed. and now that he has, would he continue to?

not that i am letting him go anyway.

✳✳✳

[7]

the sound of thunder. a whistling pressure cooker. birds cooing. you hear them from the bathroom through and despite these noises. you smell the aloe when they step out while giving tadka to the lentils. a few hugs from behind and some gentle kisses on the nape of the neck later, they heat up the biryani from last night. the latest mani ratnam movie plays on prime as you sit for lunch.

you see them eyeing you in between dollops of rice and a scene of silent on-screen romance but keep quiet. until of course, both realise. in the laughter that follows, there is as much love as there is gratitude.

who said romance was dead?

whoever did it needs to spend a day with you both. not that you complete each other's sentences or have a tucking-the-other into-bed ritual. but you just are the way you are, and romance isn't a thing either of you is actively trying to generate.

you are not trying, and that's what it is, i suppose. the secret ingredients, the magic glue; call it what you will.

if someone decided to film you guys, ever wonder what they would see?

shah rukh once said in an interview about how real love doesn't translate well on screen, and while it is easy to understand why, spending some time looking at you both transports one for a few seconds before you realize you are looking at two people that are real and not cinema.

whether it is the way you look at them, stare at them, and they stare back, or them immediately realizing that you are falling into one of your melancholic moods and playing your favorite song to dance to, i can't pinpoint. but if someone asks me about love, i am going to think about deb and meera.

i am going to think about the many things that could have gone otherwise and didn't. about things that could have made this the tragedy of dreams, and yet, how two people kept at it and kept going.

about how much of the love we seek is about perseverance.

***

You Write. We Publish.

To publish your own book, contact us.

We publish poetry collections, short story collections, novellas and novels.

contact@thewriteorder.com

Instagram- thewriteorder

www.facebook.com/thewriteorder

www.ingramcontent.com/pod-product-compliance
Lightning Source LLC
LaVergne TN
LVHW041946070526
838199LV00051BA/2925